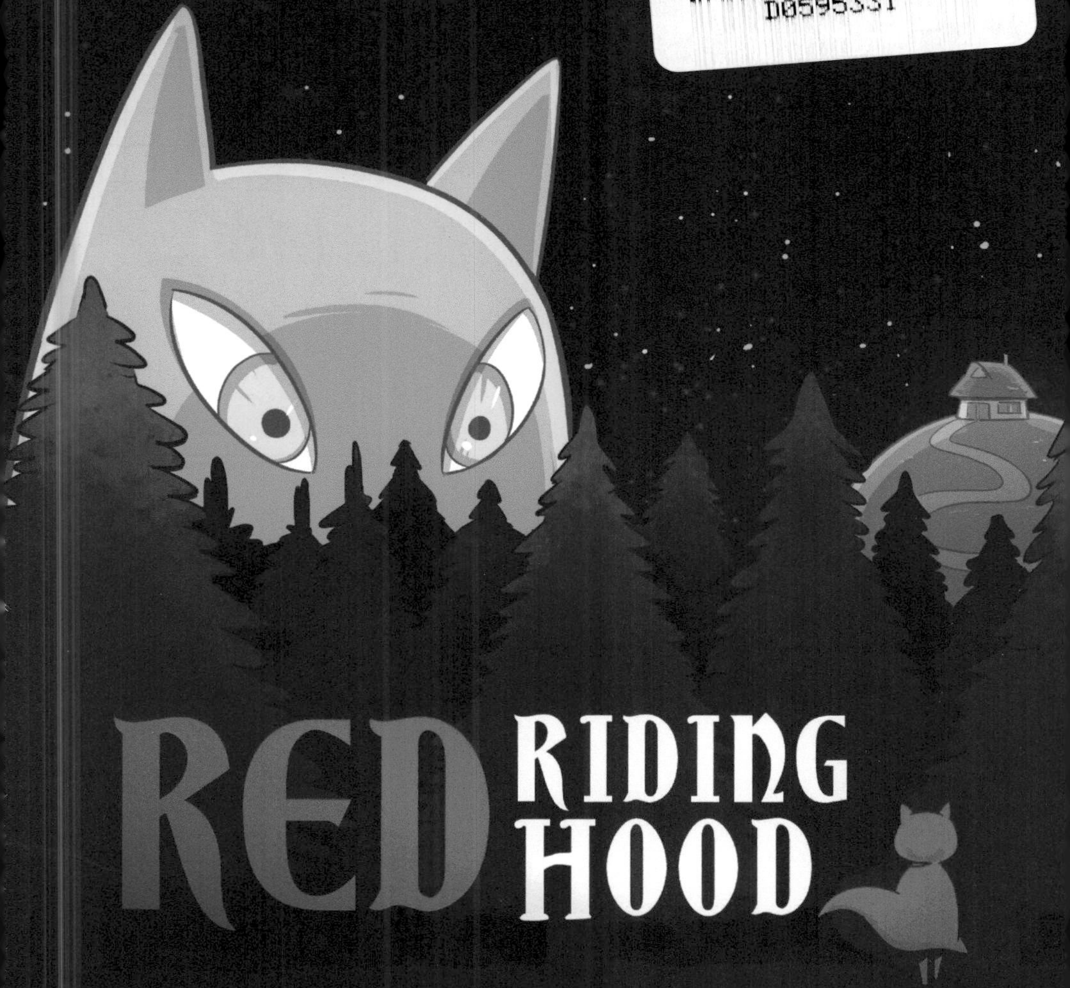

RED RIDING HOOD

BY CRISTINA OXTRA

ILLUSTRATED BY MIGUEL DÍAZ RIVAS

PICTURE WINDOW BOOKS
a capstone imprint

Discover Graphics is published by Picture Window Books,
an imprint of Capstone.
1710 Roe Crest Drive
North Mankato, Minnesota 56003
www.capstonepub.com

Library of Congress Cataloging-in-Publication Data is available on the Library of Congress website.
ISBN: 978-1-5158-7121-7 (library binding)
ISBN: 978-1-5158-7275-7 (paperback)
ISBN: 978-1-5158-7128-6 (ebook PDF)

Summary: Revisit the tale of Red Riding Hood. A visit to her grandmother turns dangerous when a wolf shows up! Will Red Riding Hood make it there safely, or fall victim to the wolf's traps?

Editorial Credits
Editor: Mari Bolte; Designer: Kay Fraser; Media Researcher: Tracy Cummins; Production Specialist: Katy LaVigne

WORDS TO KNOW

errand—a short journey to deliver or collect something

moon cake—a round pastry filled with sweet red bean or lotus seed paste; may also contain salted duck egg yolk; moon cakes are usually eaten with tea

steamed bun—a type of bread filled with meat, spices, and vegetables or sweet bean paste, sesame paste, or custard

woodsman—a person who lives or works in the woods, such as a forester, hunter, or woodcutter

Printed in the United States 4896

CAST OF CHARACTERS

Red is a kind, confident, and curious girl.

Red's **mother** enjoys cooking and baking, and wants to keep Red safe.

Red's **grandmother** is a quick thinker and skilled at sewing.

The **woodsman** is young, strong, and brave.

Beware of the **wolf**! He is sneaky, dishonest, and always hungry.

HOW TO READ A GRAPHIC NOVEL

Graphic novels are easy to read. Boxes called panels show you how to follow the story. Look at the panels from left to right and top to bottom.

Read the word boxes and word balloons from left to right as well. Don't forget the sound and action words in the pictures.

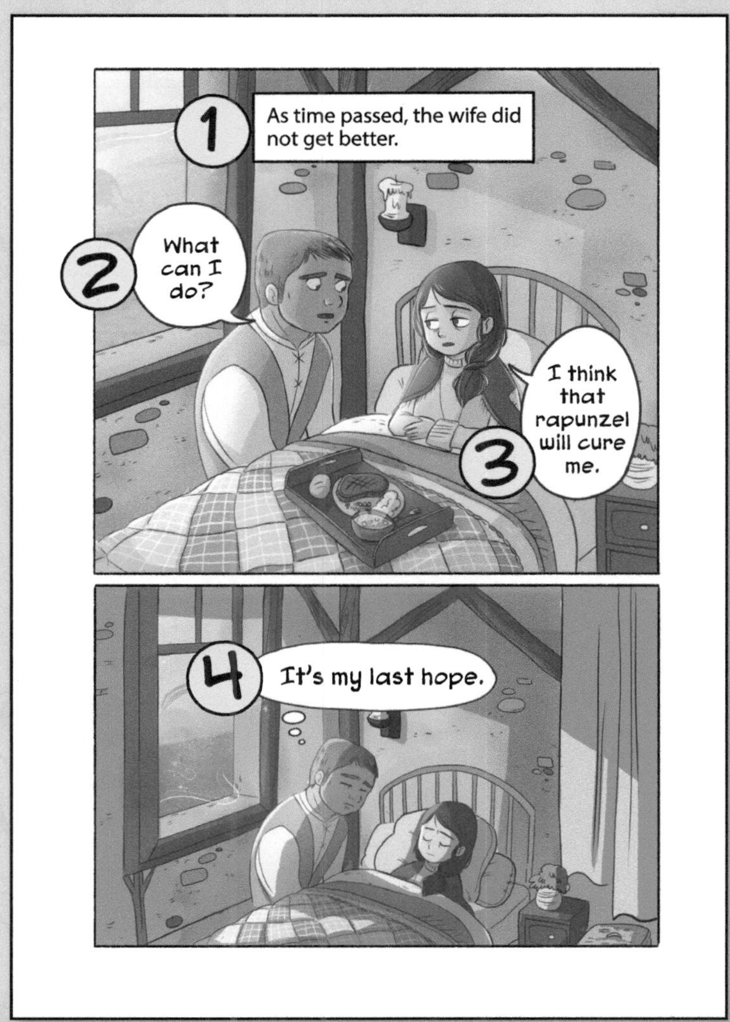
1
As time passed, the wife did not get better.
2
What can I do?
3
I think that rapunzel will cure me.
4
It's my last hope.

The pictures and the words work together to tell the whole story.

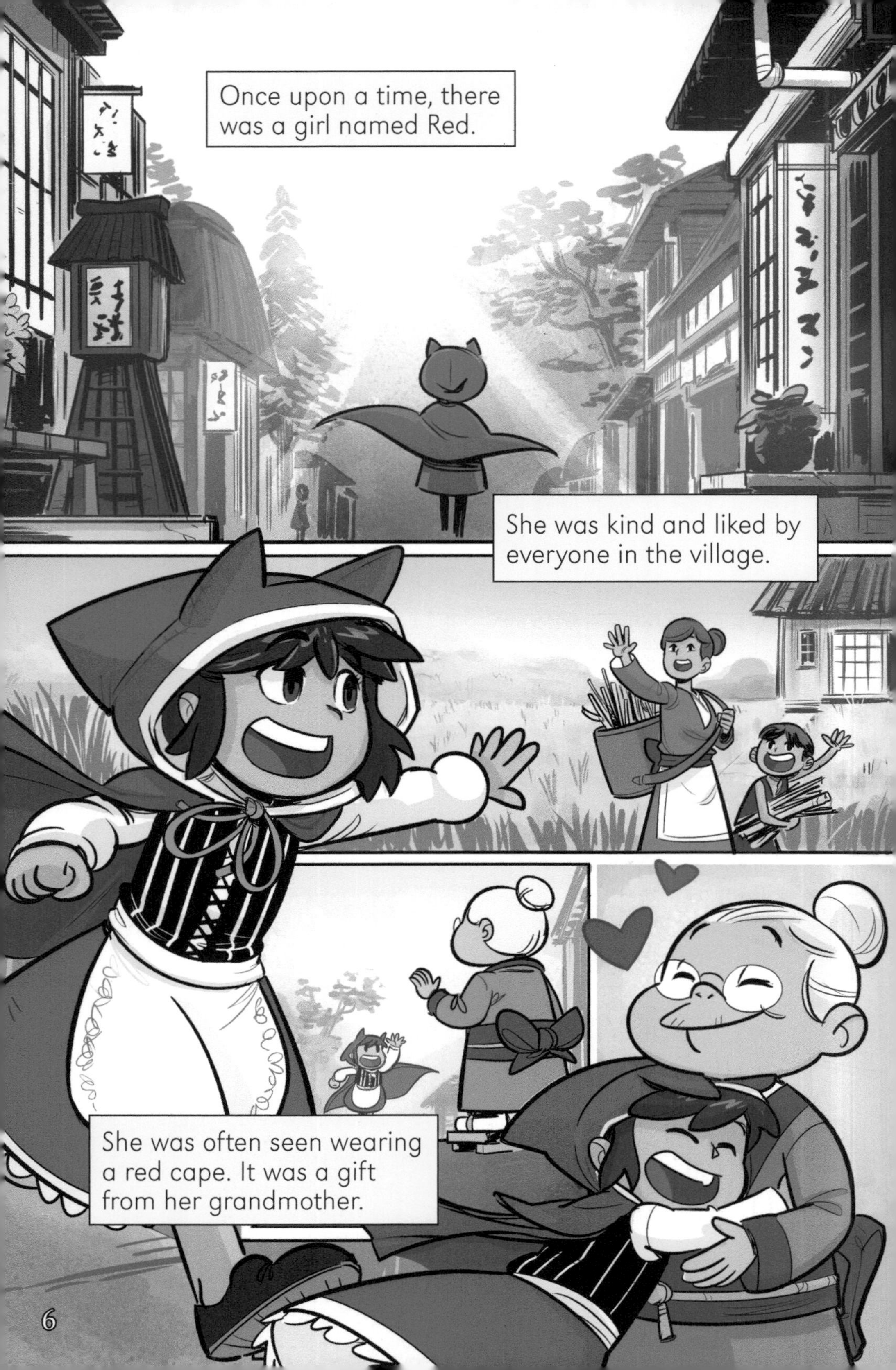
Once upon a time, there was a girl named Red.
She was kind and liked by everyone in the village.
She was often seen wearing a red cape. It was a gift from her grandmother.

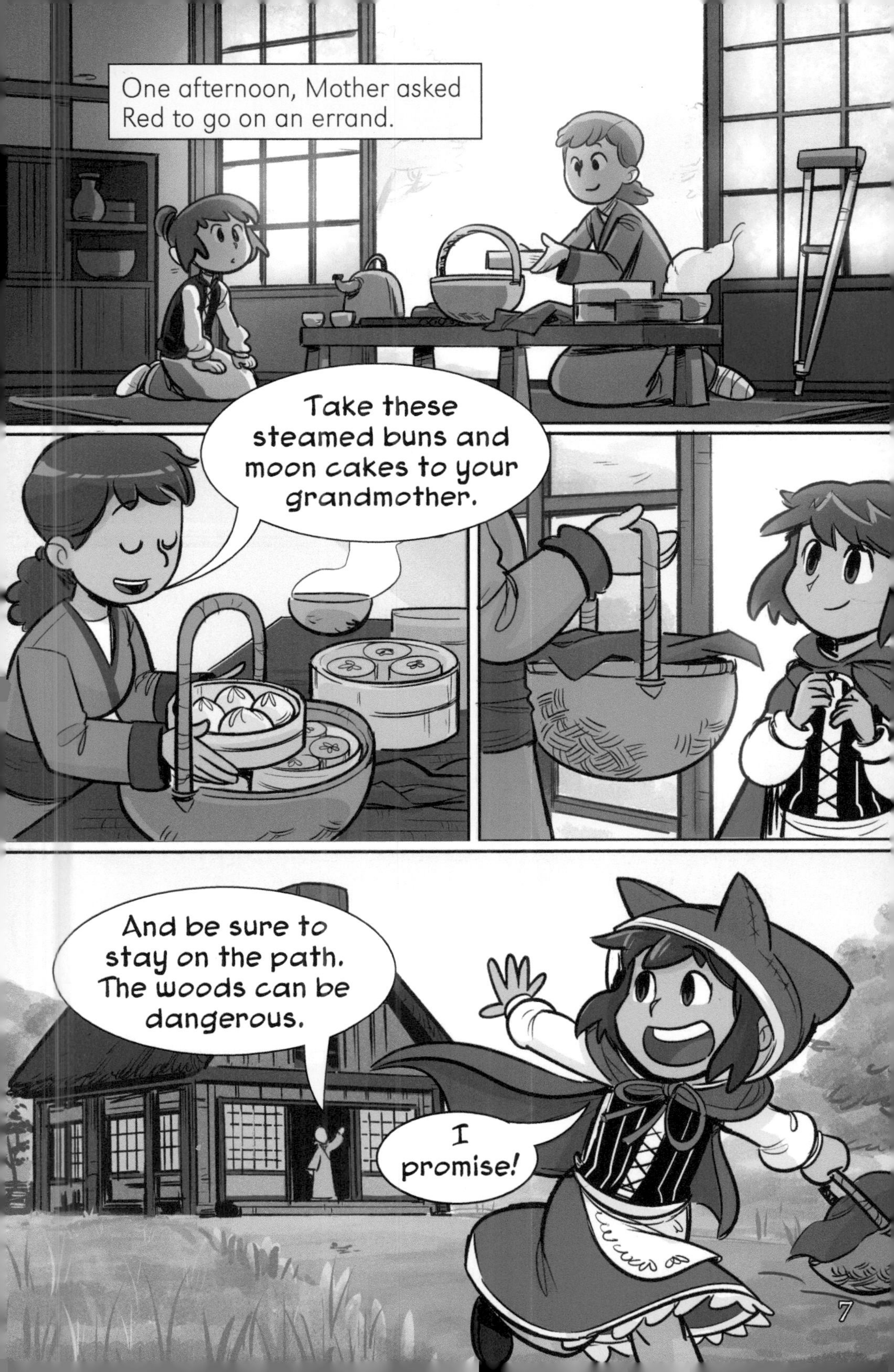
One afternoon, Mother asked Red to go on an errand.
Take these steamed buns and moon cakes to your grandmother.
And be sure to stay on the path. The woods can be dangerous.
I promise!

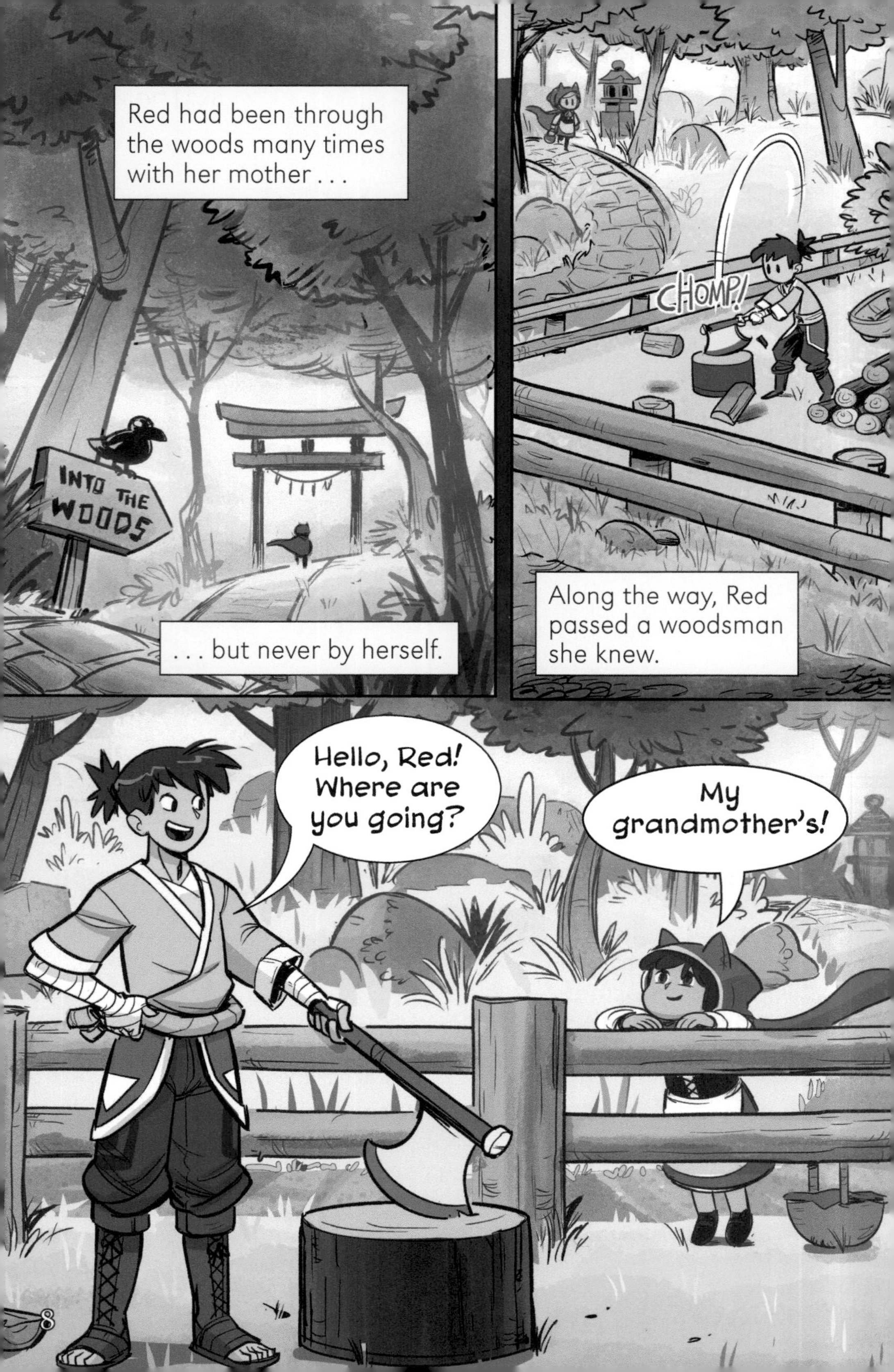
Red had been through the woods many times with her mother . . .
INTO THE WOODS
. . . but never by herself.
CHOMP!
Along the way, Red passed a woodsman she knew.
Hello, Red! Where are you going?
My grandmother's!

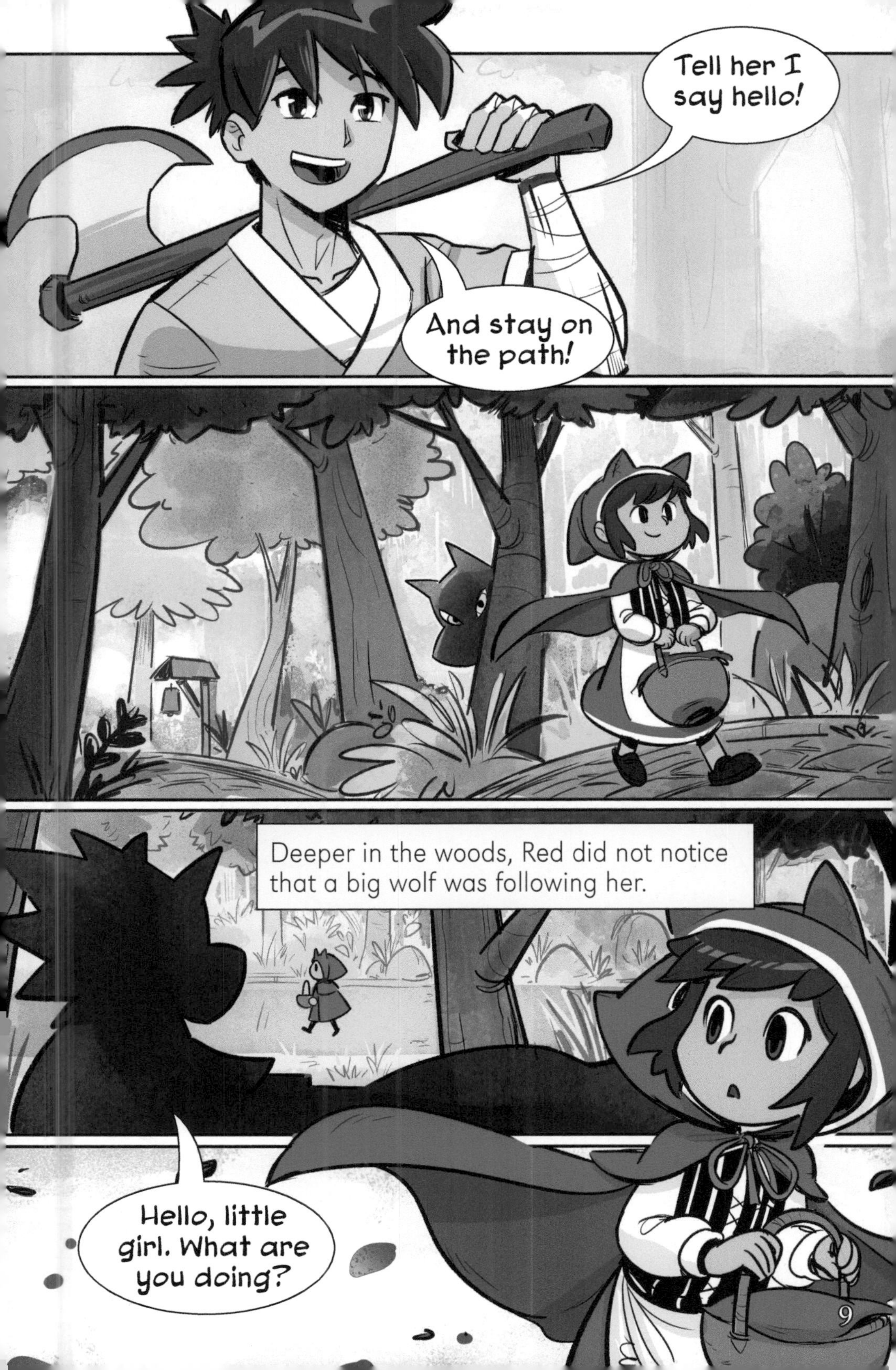
Tell her I say hello!
And stay on the path!
Deeper in the woods, Red did not notice that a big wolf was following her.
Hello, little girl. What are you doing?

I'm bringing food to my grandmother. She lives over the hill.
Really?
She might like some flowers too. There. Can you see them?

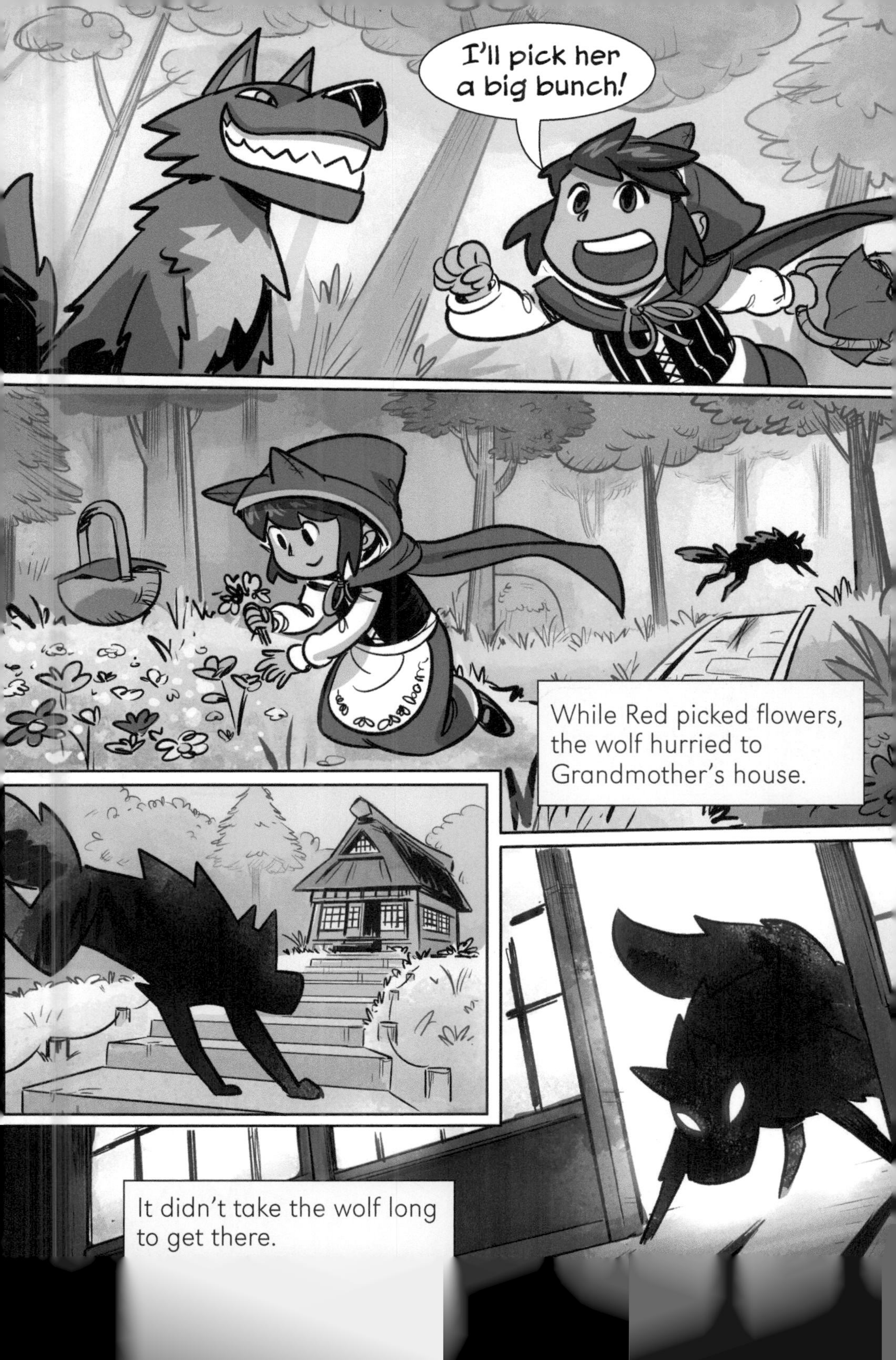
I'll pick her
a big bunch!
While Red picked flowers,
the wolf hurried to
Grandmother's house.
It didn't take the wolf long
to get there.

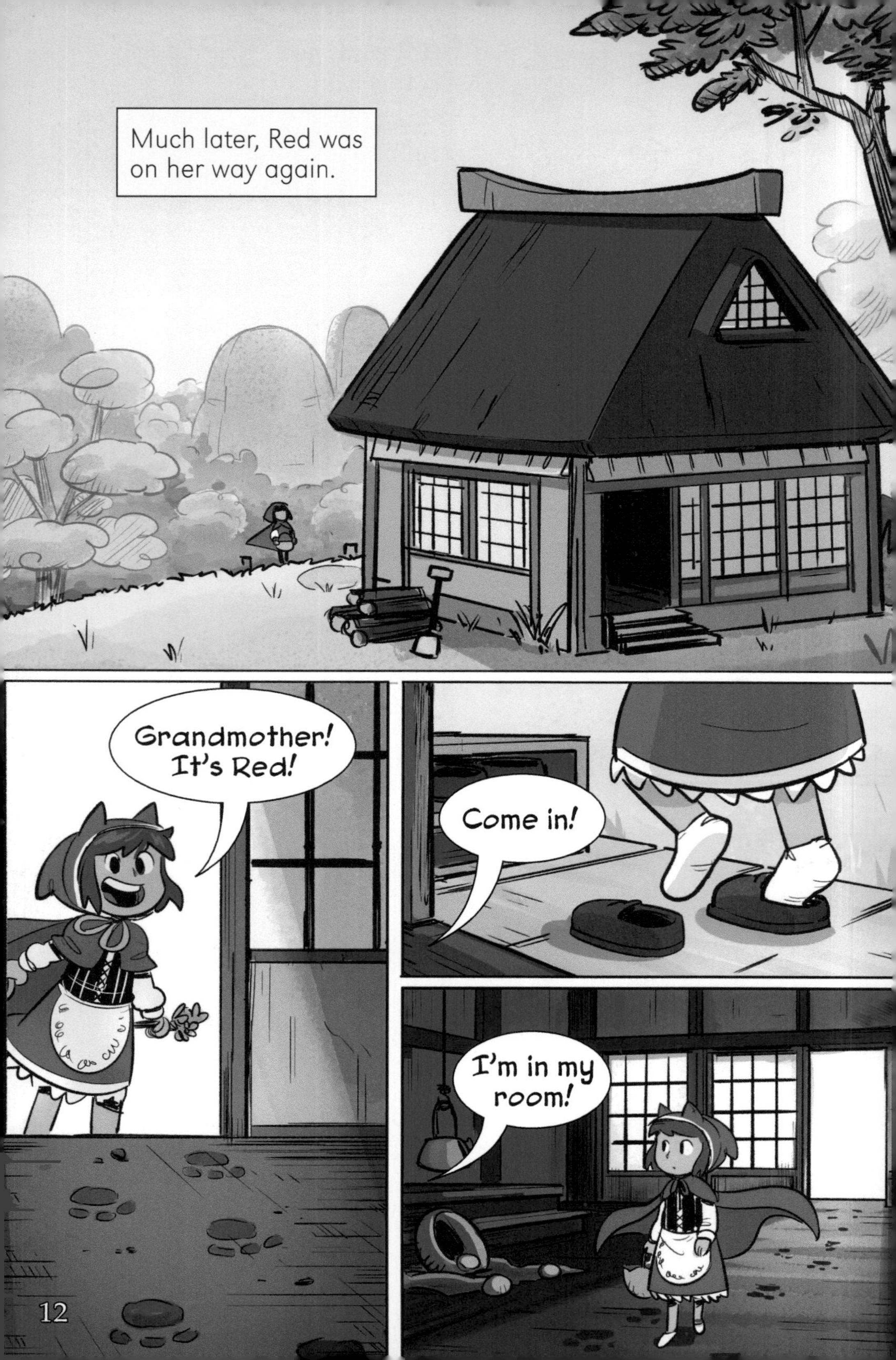
Much later, Red was on her way again.
Grandmother! It's Red!
Come in!
I'm in my room!

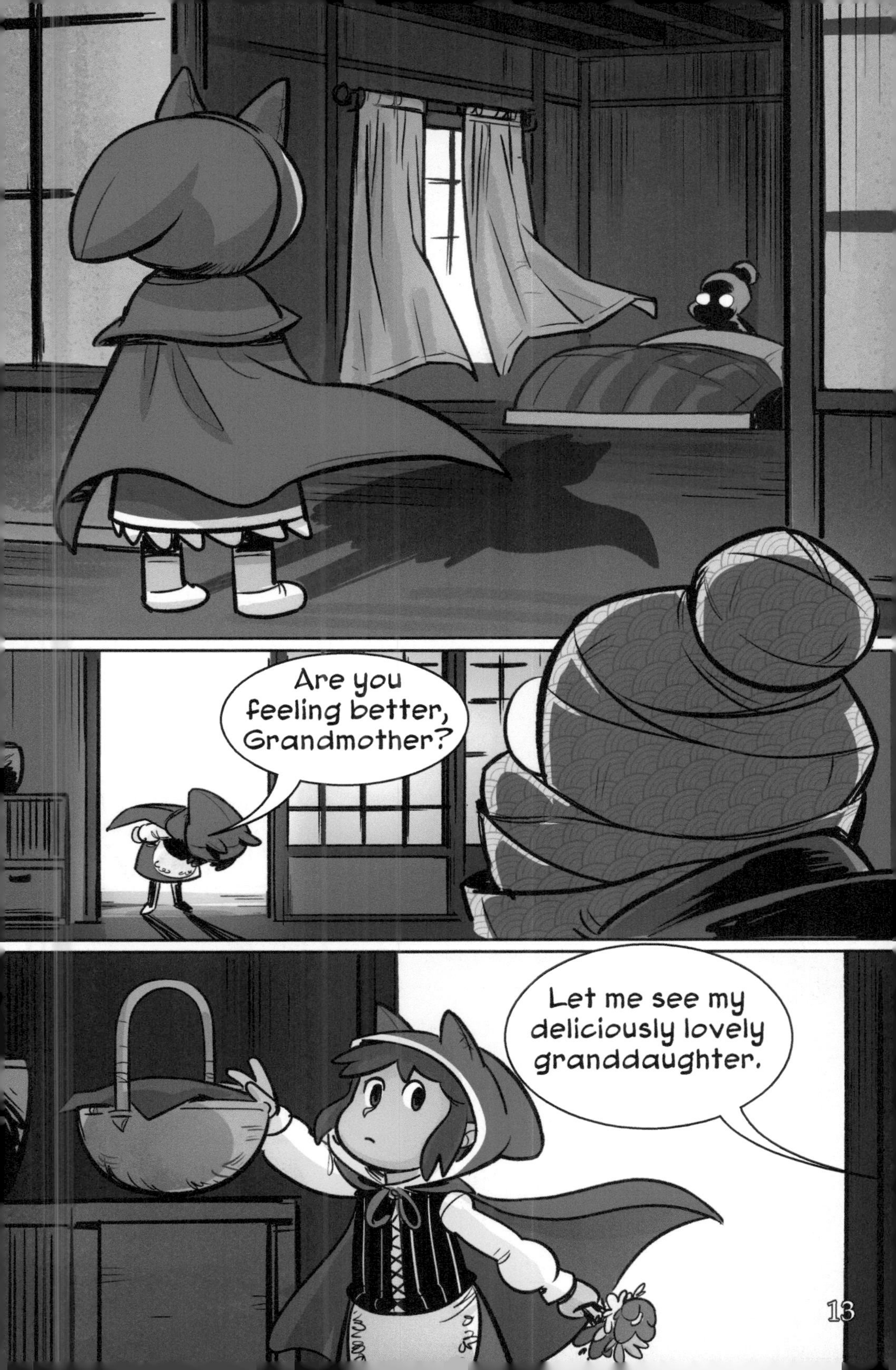
Are you feeling better, Grandmother?
Let me see my deliciously lovely granddaughter.

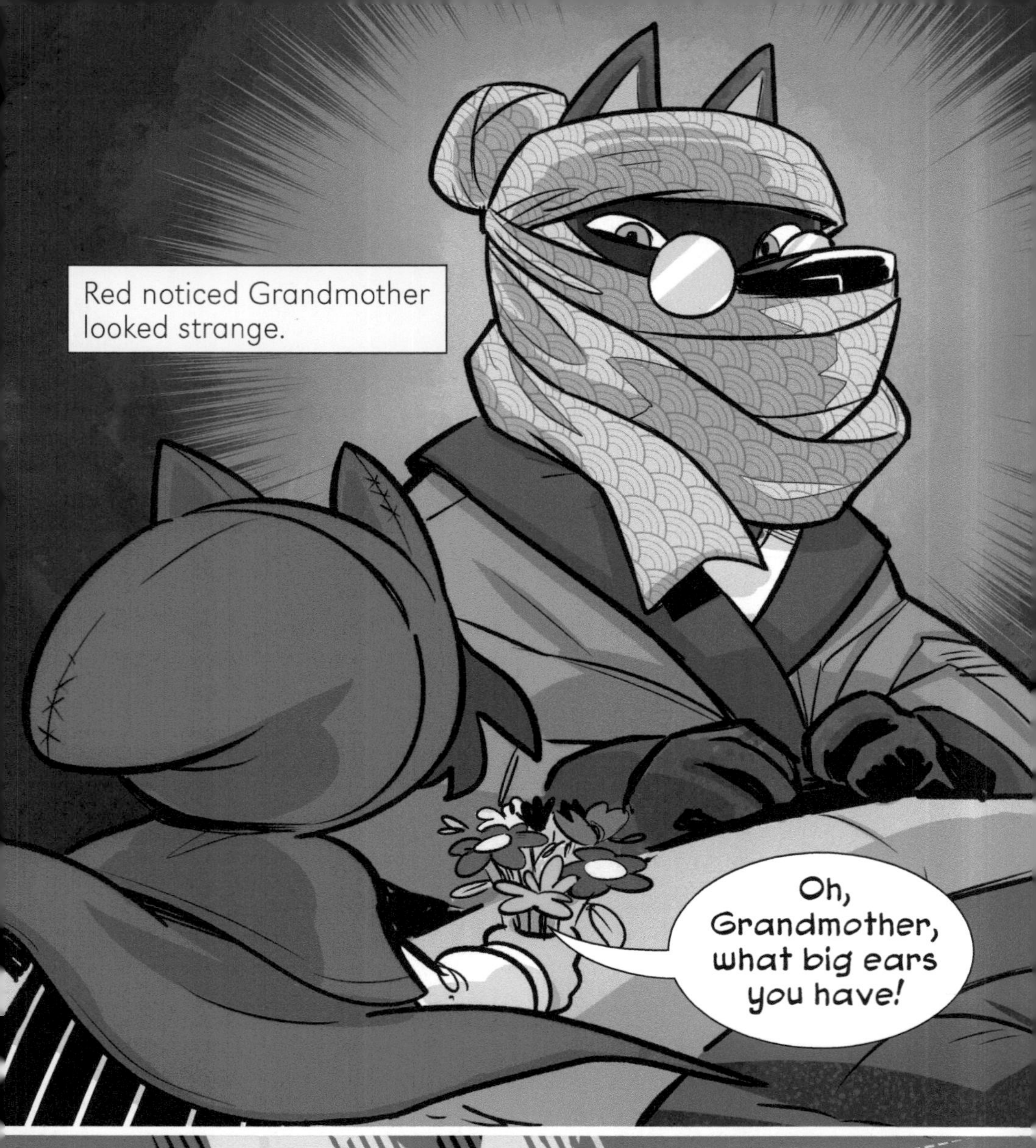

Red noticed Grandmother looked strange.
Oh, Grandmother, what big ears you have!

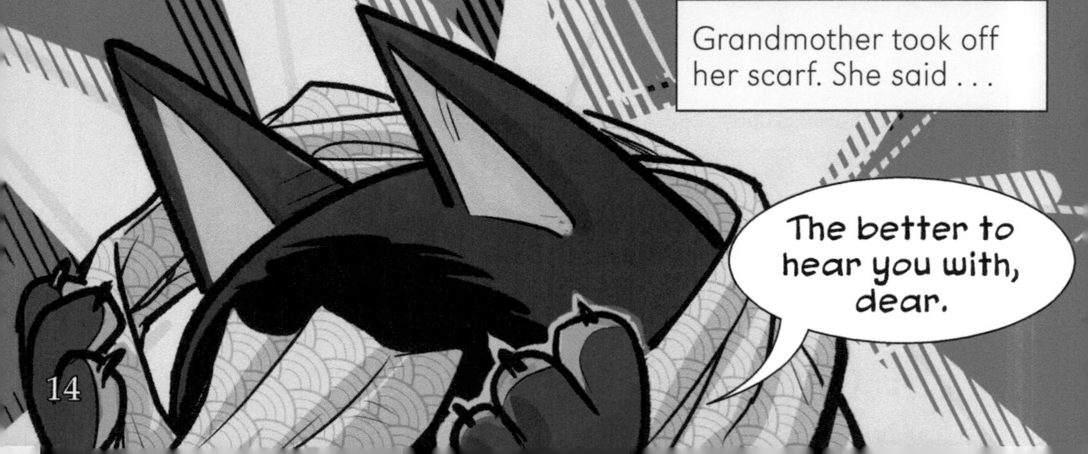

Grandmother took off her scarf. She said . . .
The better to hear you with, dear.

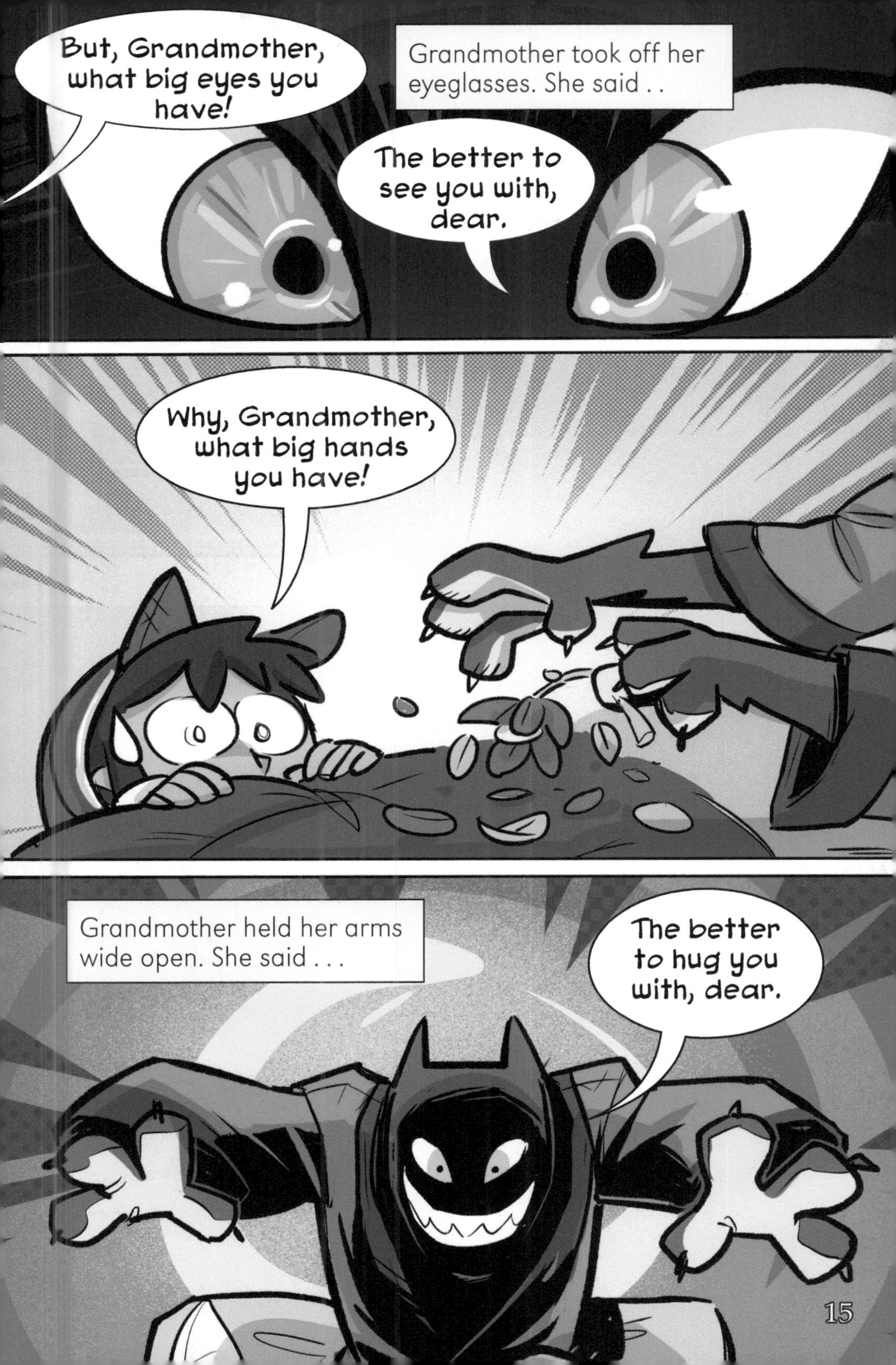
But, Grandmother, what big eyes you have!
Grandmother took off her eyeglasses. She said . .
The better to see you with, dear.
Why, Grandmother, what big hands you have!
Grandmother held her arms wide open. She said . . .
The better to hug you with, dear.

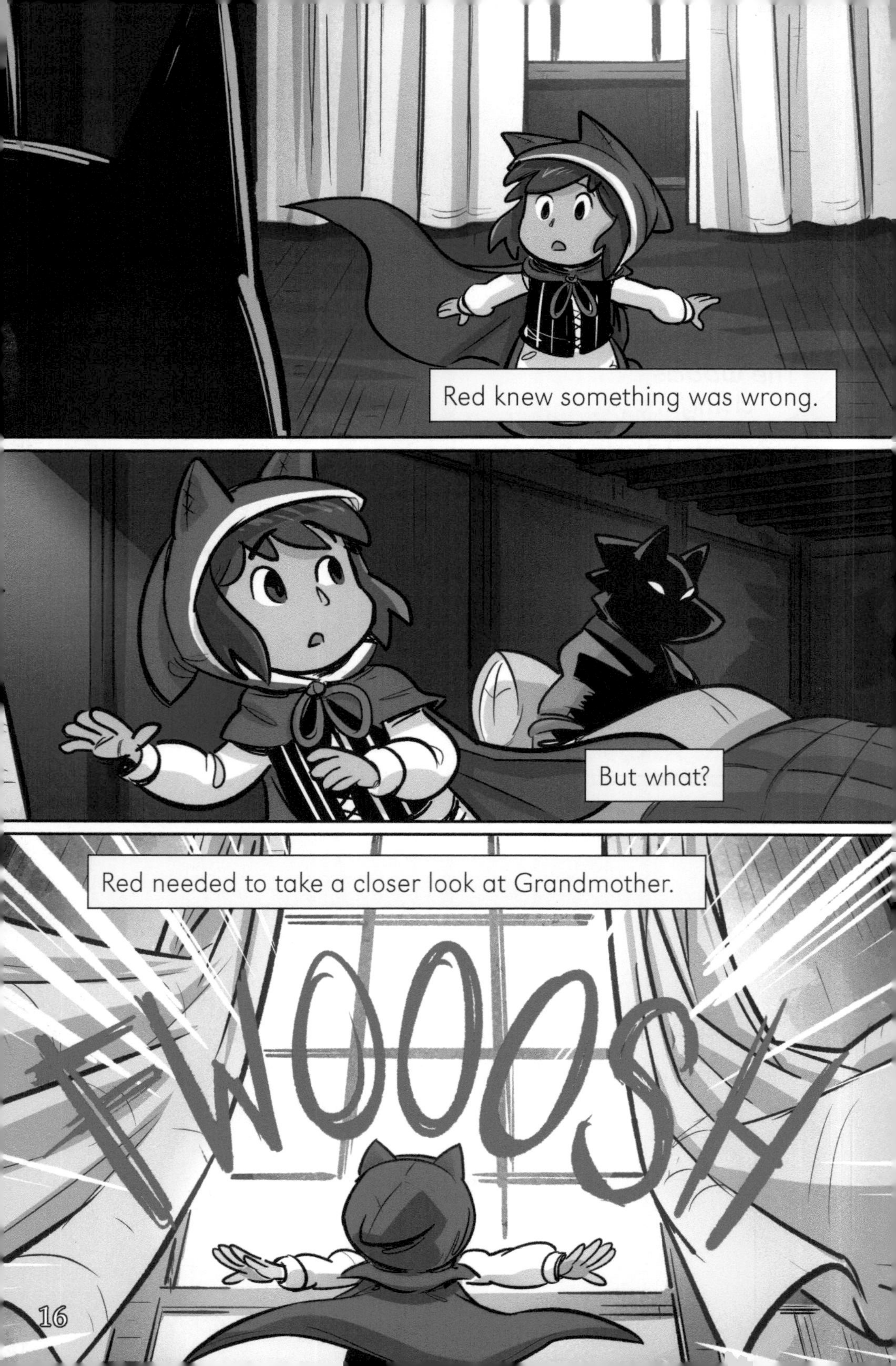
Red knew something was wrong.
But what?
Red needed to take a closer look at Grandmother.
WOOOSH

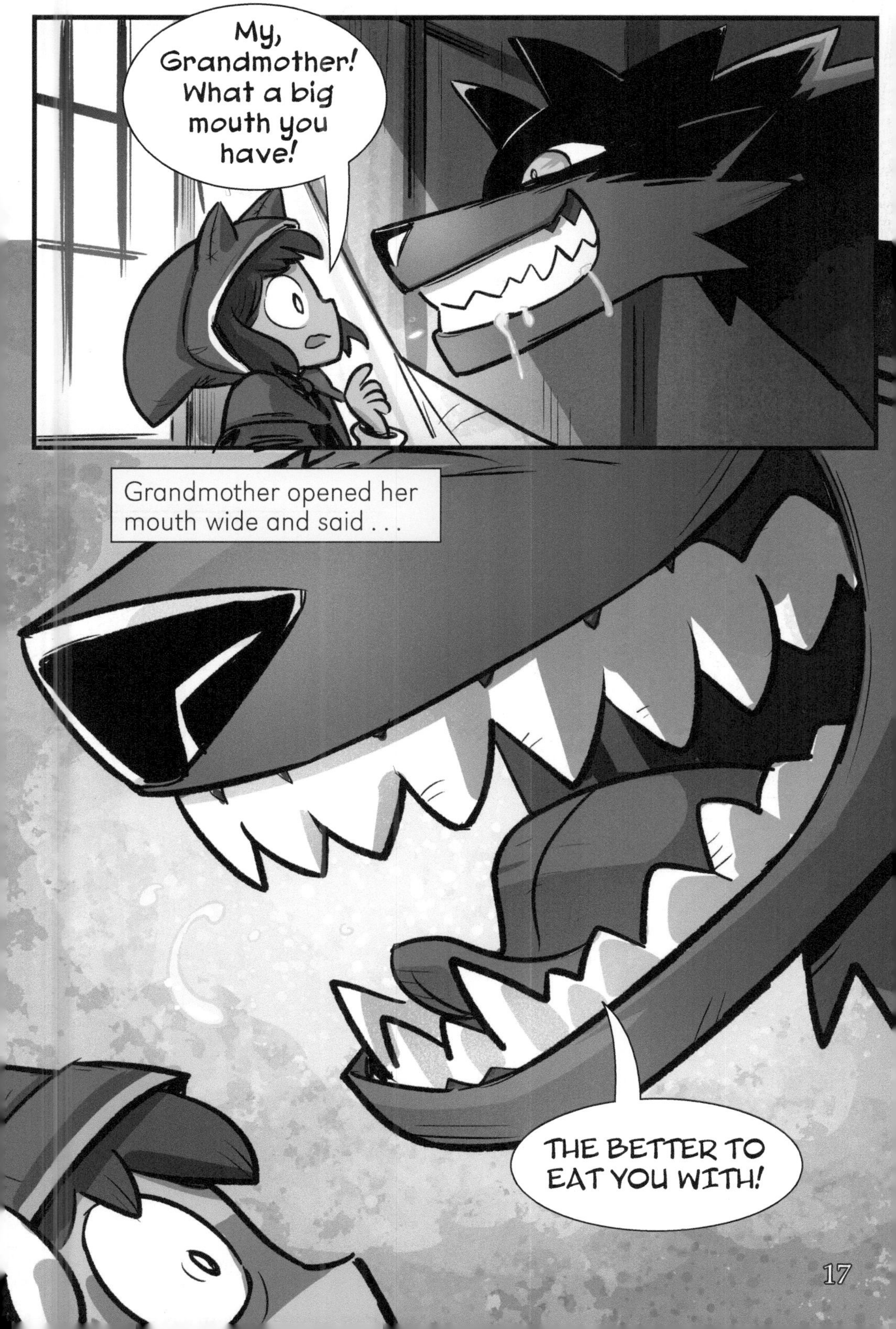
My, Grandmother! What a big mouth you have!
Grandmother opened her mouth wide and said . . .
THE BETTER TO EAT YOU WITH!

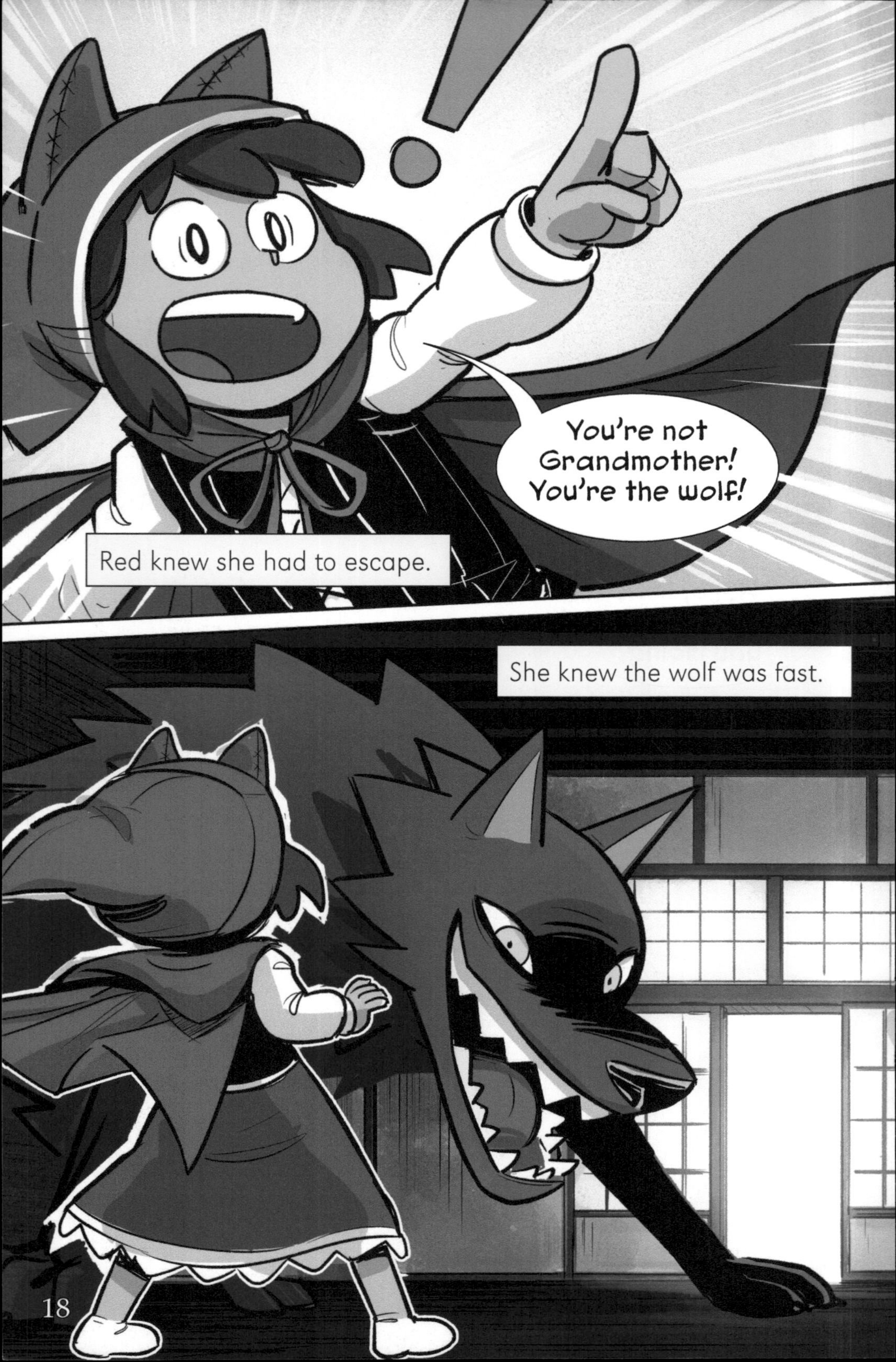
You're not Grandmother! You're the wolf!
Red knew she had to escape.
She knew the wolf was fast.

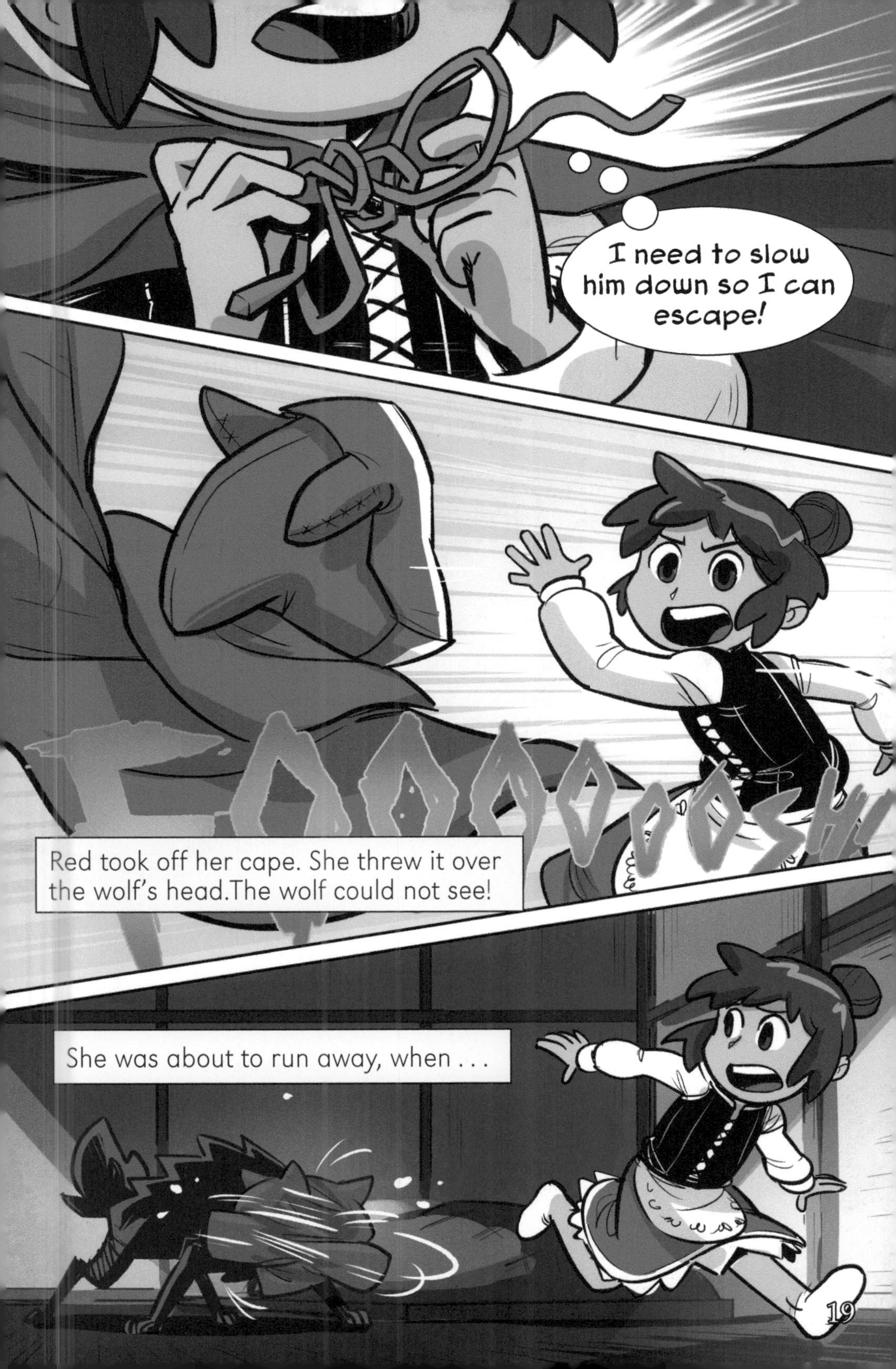
I need to slow him down so I can escape!
FOOOOOSH!
Red took off her cape. She threw it over the wolf's head.The wolf could not see!
She was about to run away, when . . .

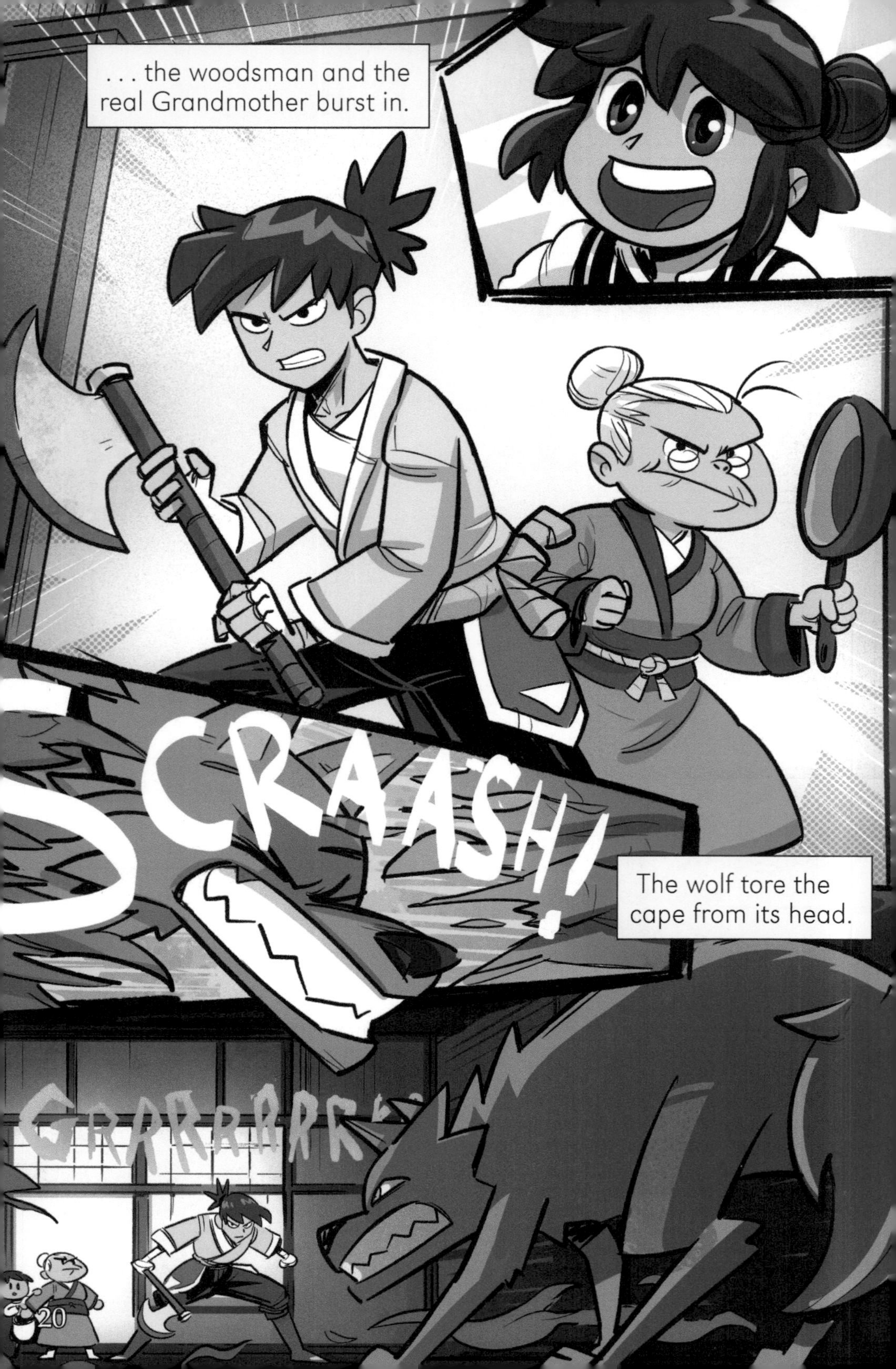

. . . the woodsman and the real Grandmother burst in.
SCRAASH!
The wolf tore the cape from its head.
GRRRRRRR

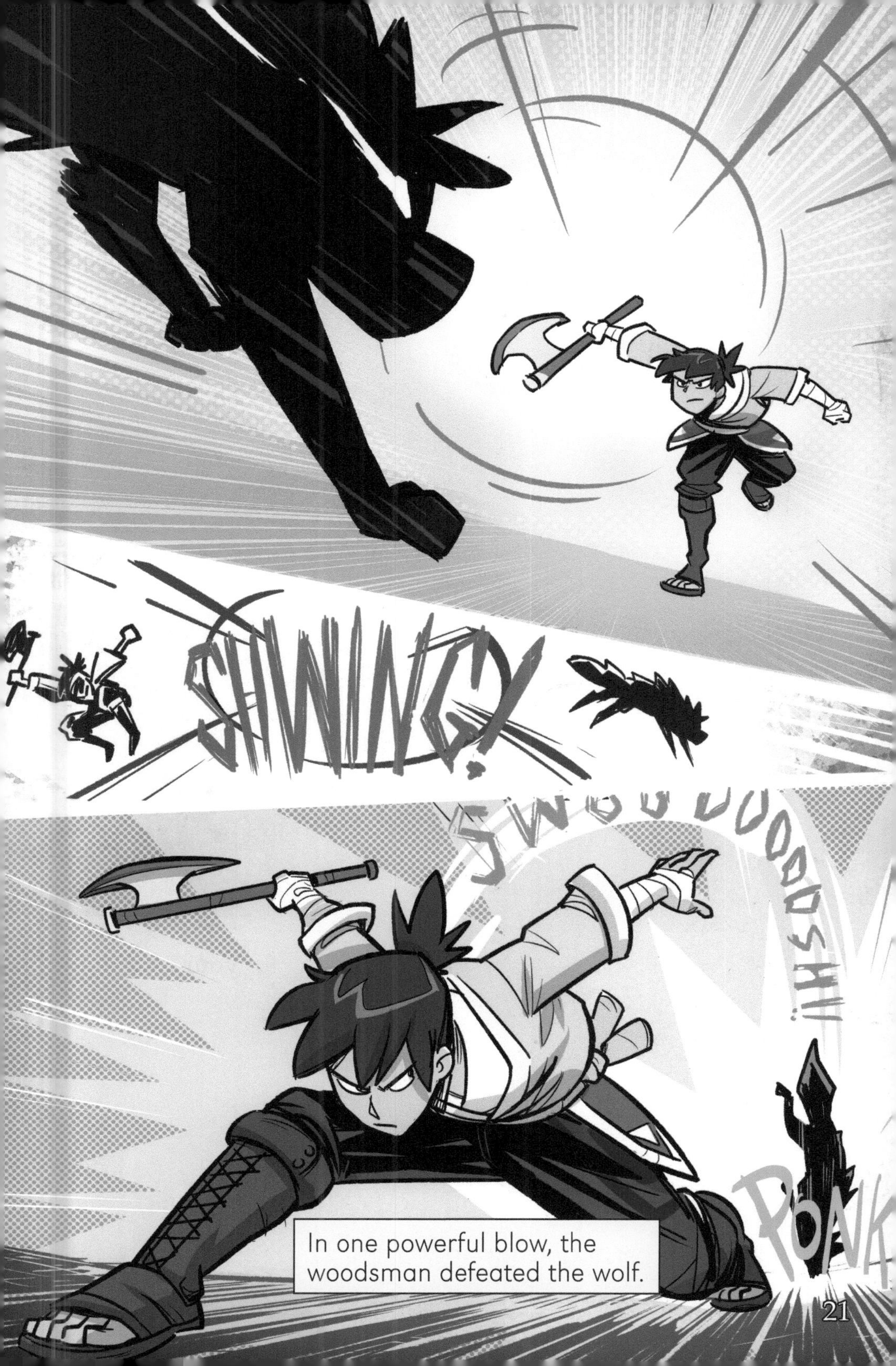
SHWING!
SWOOOOOOOOSH!!
In one powerful blow, the woodsman defeated the wolf.
PONK

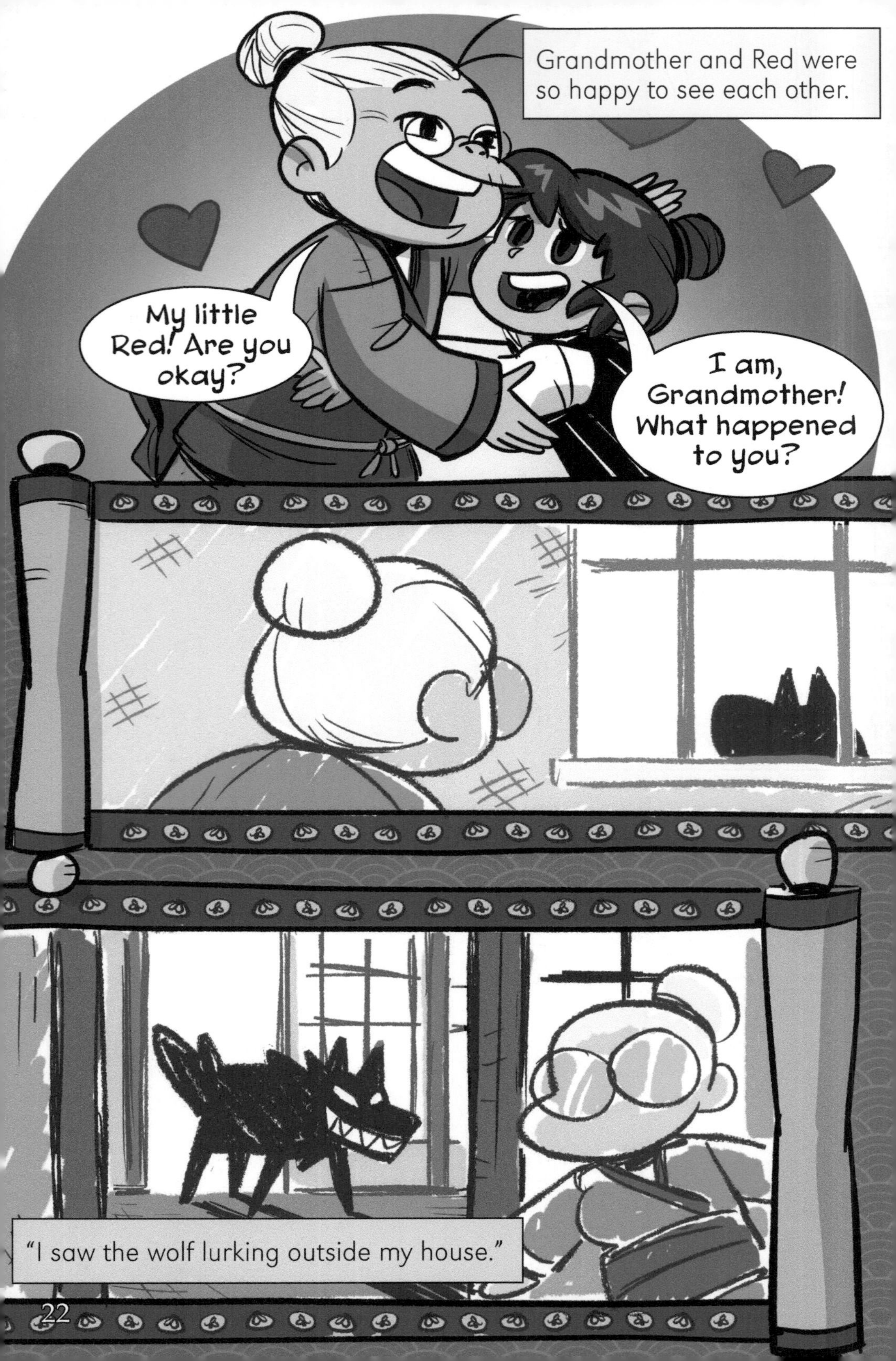
Grandmother and Red were so happy to see each other.
My little Red! Are you okay?
I am, Grandmother! What happened to you?
"I saw the wolf lurking outside my house."

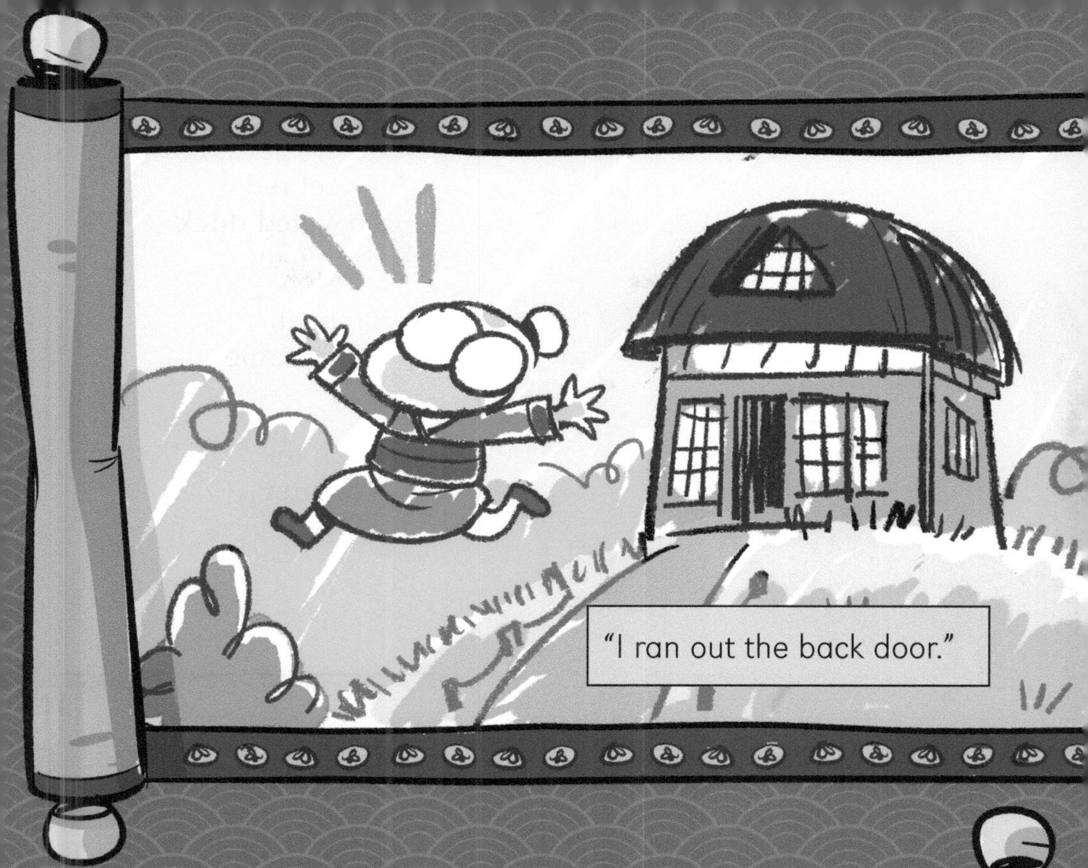
"I ran out the back door."

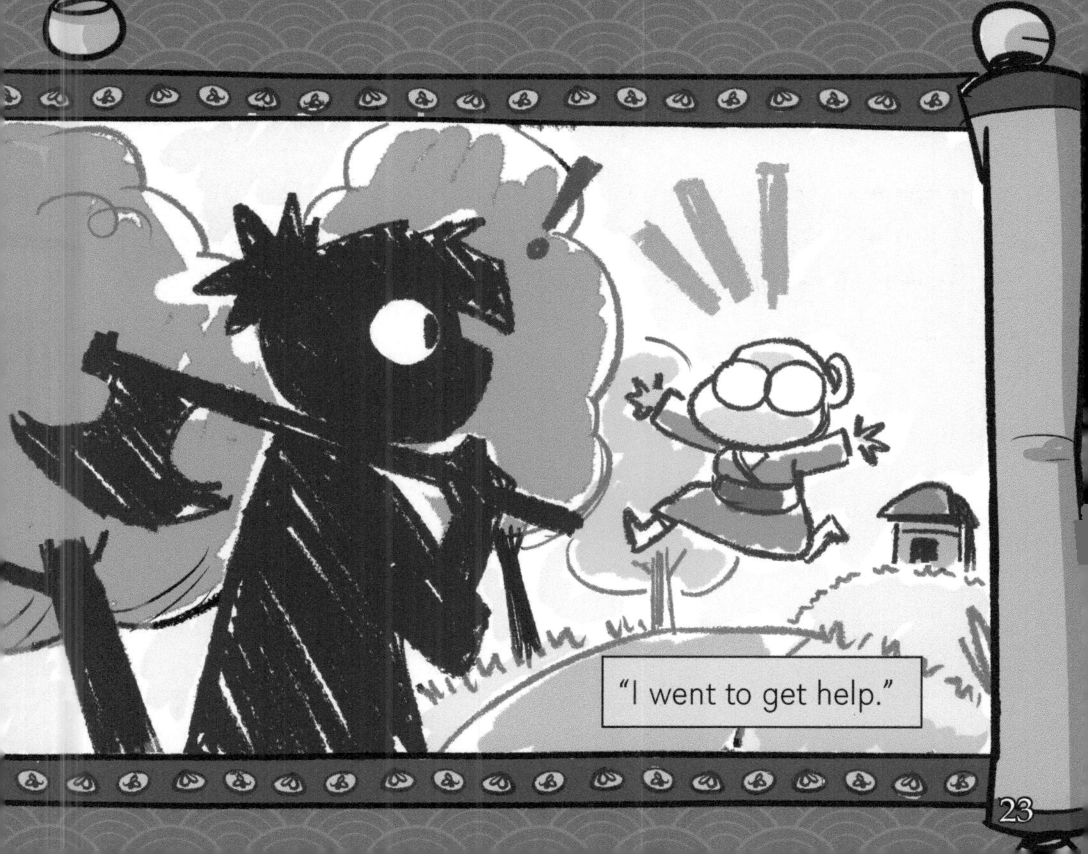
"I went to get help."

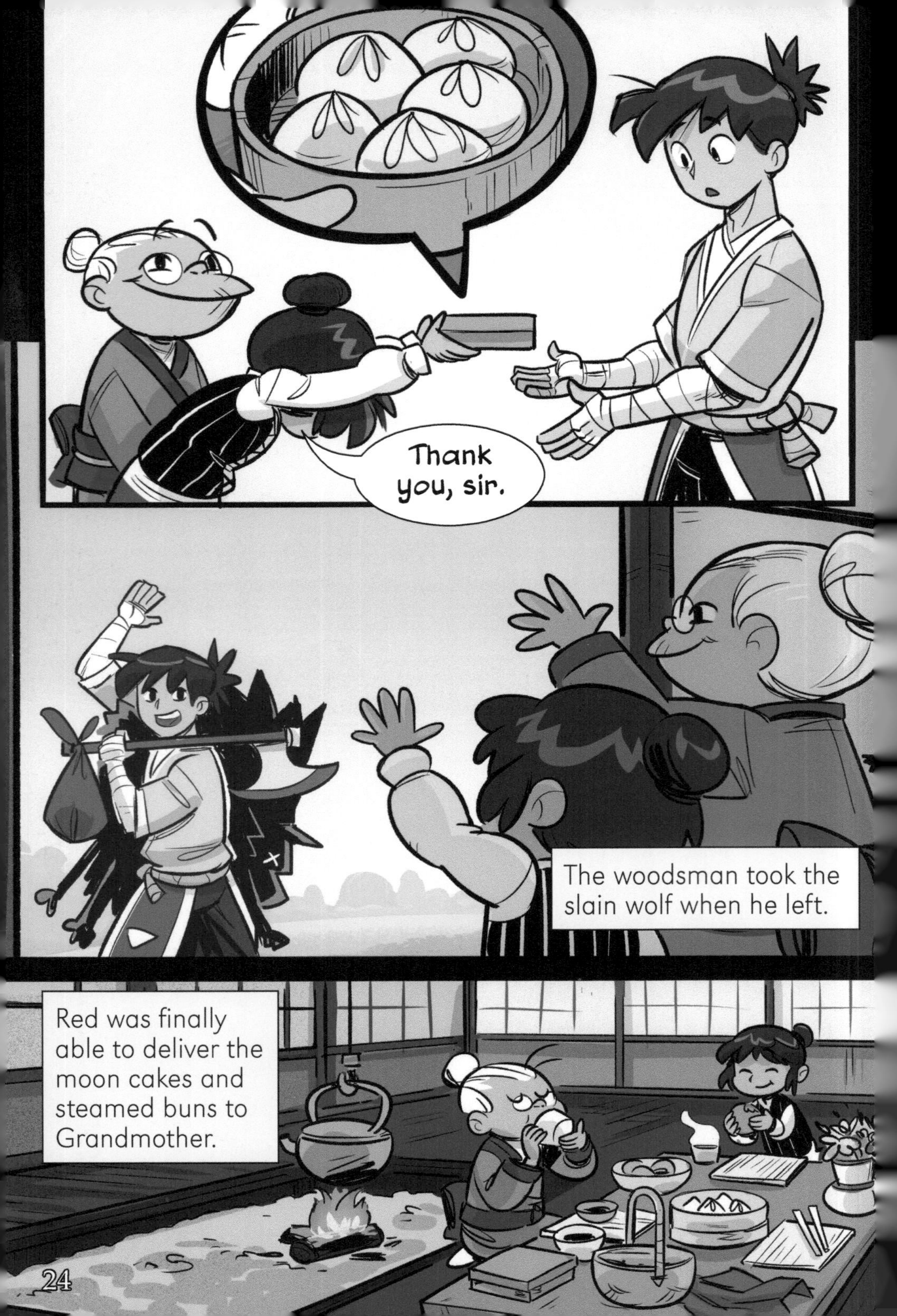
Thank you, sir.
The woodsman took the slain wolf when he left.
Red was finally able to deliver the moon cakes and steamed buns to Grandmother.

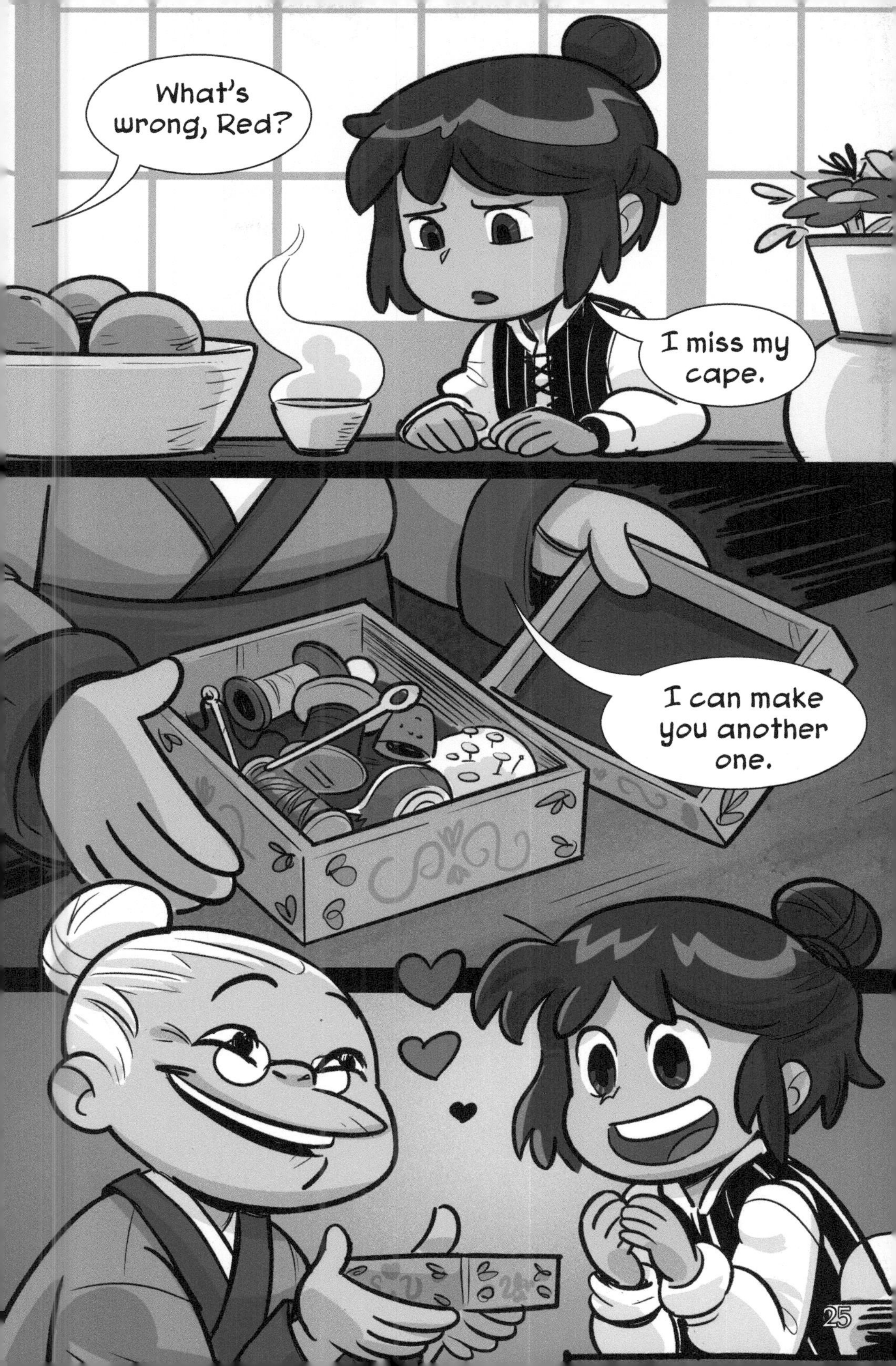
What's wrong, Red?
I miss my cape.
I can make you another one.

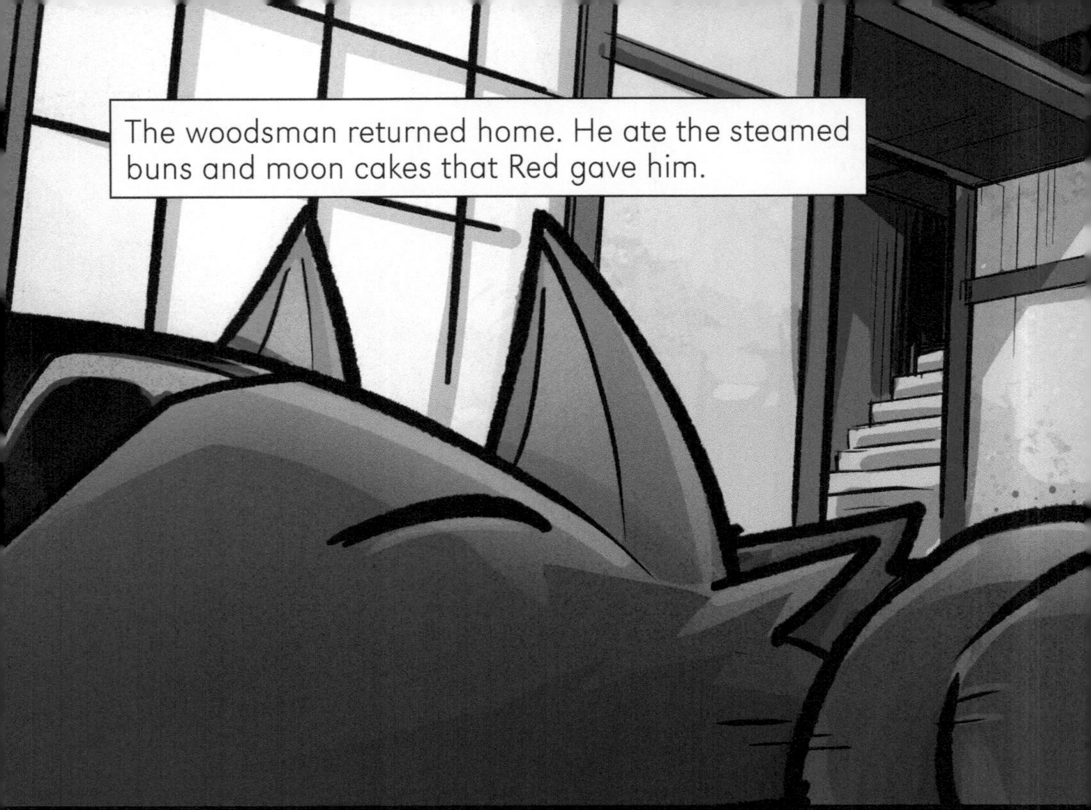
The woodsman returned home. He ate the steamed buns and moon cakes that Red gave him.

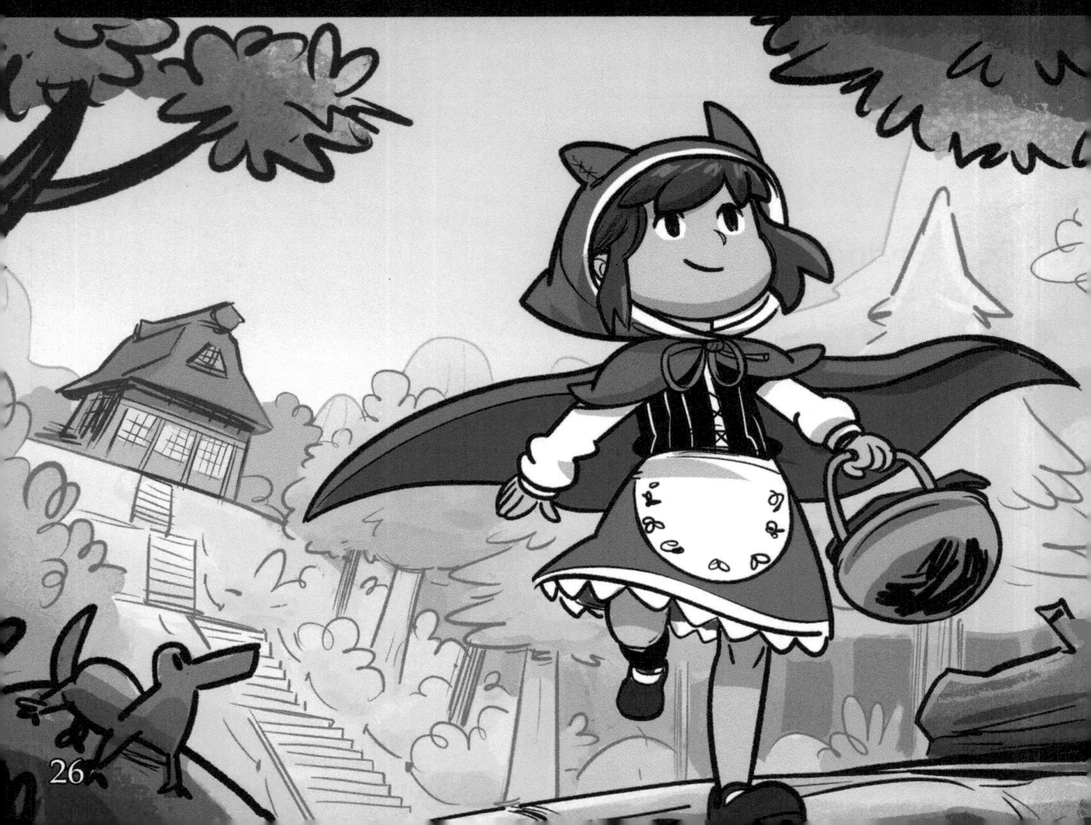

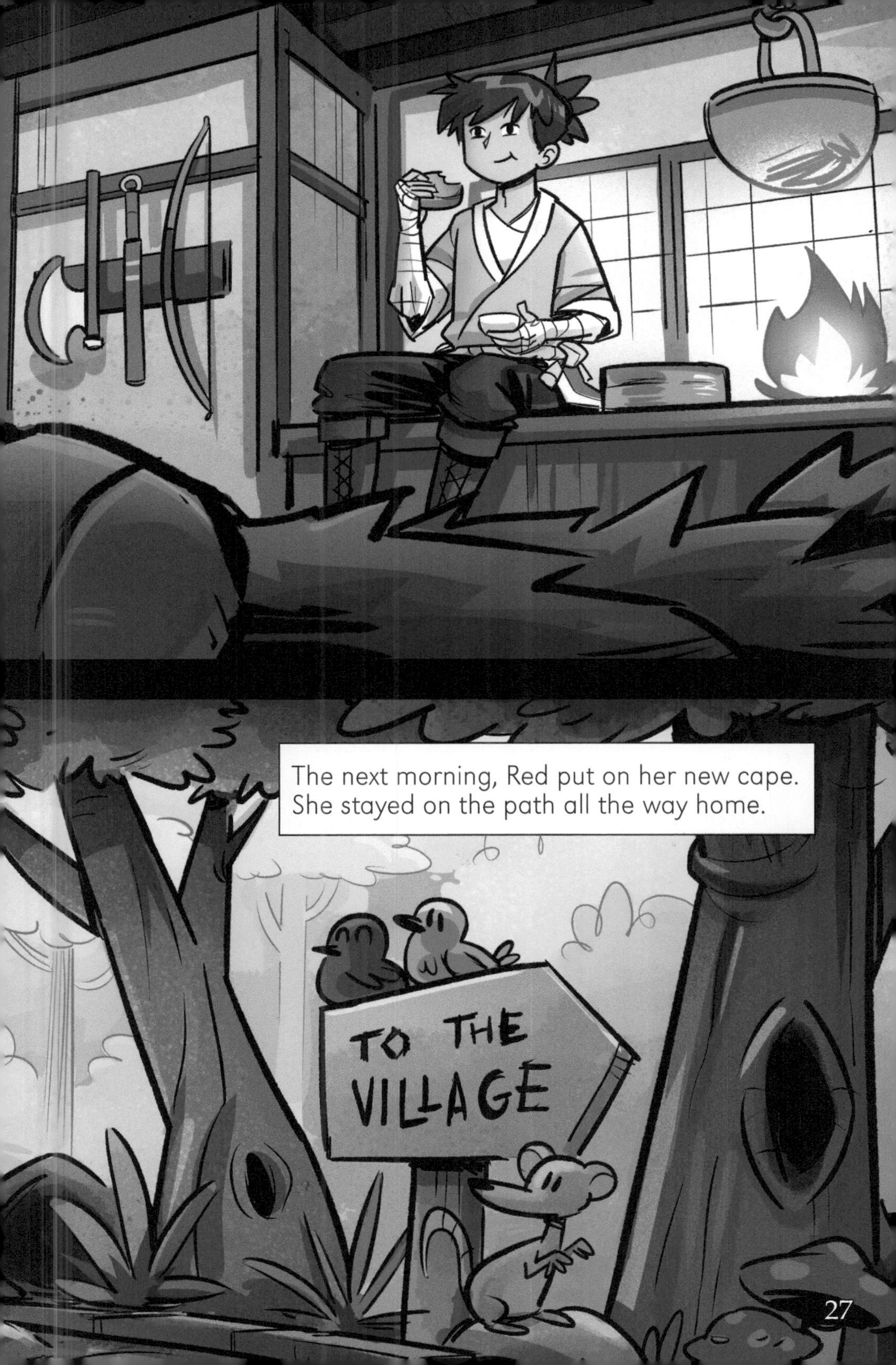
The next morning, Red put on her new cape. She stayed on the path all the way home.
TO THE VILLAGE

WRITING PROMPTS

1. How do you think the story would have ended if Red had met a deer or a rabbit instead of a wolf? Rewrite the story with a different animal.

2. Red packed moon cakes and steamed buns for her grandmother. What would you have packed? Make a list.

3. Retell the story from a first-person perspective, as though you are Red telling her mother what happened.

DISCUSSION QUESTIONS

1. What lesson, or lessons, does the story of Red Riding Hood teach?

2. Re-read the story. When do you think Red knew it was not Grandmother in the bed? What clues do the illustrations give you?

3. Why was it important for Red to stay on the path?

GRANDMOTHER'S BASKET

What would you have packed in the basket for your grandmother?

WHAT YOU NEED:

- crayons and markers
- brown construction paper
- scissors
- glue
- white construction paper
- magazines and newspapers

WHAT YOU DO:

Step 1: Draw a large bowl shape on the brown construction paper. This will be the basket. Draw a handle for your basket too.

Step 2: Cut out the basket and handle. Glue them onto the white construction paper.

Step 3: Look through the magazines and newspapers for pictures of food and drinks. Cut out any that you would like to add to your basket.

Step 4: Glue the food and drink cutouts to the top of the basket. This will make it look like they are inside the basket. Glue some around the basket too.

Step 5: Compare baskets with your friends. What kinds of things do they like to eat and drink? Did anyone have something you haven't tried before? Were there any items that were very popular?

READ ALL THE AMAZING BOOKS IN THIS SERIES

CINDERELLA
DISCOVER DG GRAPHICS
WRITTEN BY JENNIFER FANDEL ILLUSTRATED BY MICHELLE SIMPSON

BEAUTY and the BEAST
DISCOVER DG GRAPHICS
WRITTEN BY JESSICA GUNDERSON ILLUSTRATED BY THAIS DAMIÃO

RAPUNZEL
DISCOVER DG GRAPHICS
WRITTEN BY JENNIFER FANDEL ILLUSTRATED BY ANUKI LOPEZ

SLEEPING BEAUTY
DISCOVER DG GRAPHICS
WRITTEN BY JESSICA GUNDERSON ILLUSTRATED BY RUSS COX

HANSEL AND GRETEL
DISCOVER DG GRAPHICS
WRITTEN BY JESSICA GUNDERSON ILLUSTRATED BY ALEX LOPEZ

DISCOVER DG GRAPHICS
RED RIDING HOOD
WRITTEN BY CRISTINA OXTRA ILLUSTRATED BY MIGUEL DÍAZ RIVAS

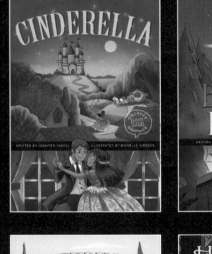

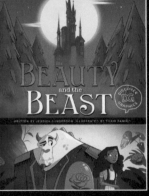